Saving Ethan

Kaci Rose

Five Little Roses Publishing

Copyright

Copyright © 2022, by Kaci Rose, Five Little Roses Publishing. All Rights Reserved.

No part of this publication may be reproduced, distributed, or transmitted in any form or by any means, including photocopying, recording, or other electronic or mechanical methods, or by any information storage and retrieval system without the prior written permission of the publisher, except in the case of very brief quotations embodied in critical reviews and certain other noncommercial uses permitted by copyright law.

Publisher's Note: This is a work of fiction. Names, characters, places, and incidents are a product of the author's imagination. Locales and public names are sometimes used for atmospheric purposes. Any resemblance to actual people, living or dead, or to businesses, companies, events, institutions, or locales is completely coincidental.

Book Cover By: **Comar Covers**
Editing By: **Violet Rae**

Dedication

To all the men and women serving our country, past and present. To their friends and families who support them daily.

Blurb

She's a high school sweetheart. He's back in town looking after being discharged from the military. Is he ready for the huge secret she's been keeping from him?

Bri
Ethan was my everything growing up, my first everything, my best friend, and my soul mate. Until he walked away and ended us.

We had one last beautiful night together and then he was gone.

That night gave me our son. The problem is Ethans is back in town, and he doesn't know about our little boy...

Ethan
Leaving her was the hardest thing I've ever done but it was the right thing to do. She didn't have a future with me.

I was planning to make the Navy my whole life until I was injured and discharged.

Having to start all over I pack up and head home to my parents.

Walking into the diner that first morning I never thought I'd see her.

The only woman I'd ever loved but the biggest shocker? The little boy sitting next to her is the spitting image of me...

Contents

Get Free Books!	IX
1. Chapter 1	1
2. Chapter 2	8
3. Chapter 3	13
4. Chapter 4	18
5. Chapter 5	24
6. Chapter 6	28
7. Chapter 7	33
8. Chapter 8	38
9. Chapter 9	43
10. Chapter 10	49
11. Chapter 11	53
12. Epilogue	56
Other Books by Kaci Rose	60
Connect with Kaci Rose	63
About Kaci Rose	65

Please Leave a Review!

Get Free Books!

Do you like Military Men? Best friends brothers?
What about sweet, sexy, and addicting books?

If you join Kaci Rose's Newsletter you get these books free!

**https://www.kacirose.com/free-books/
Now on to the story!**

Chapter 1

Briana

Five Years ago

What a rush to finally graduate high school. I'm officially an adult, even though I've been eighteen for six months. It's the final piece of the puzzle of stepping into the adult world.

My entire future is before me, even more so since my boyfriend Ethan has asked me to meet with him tonight. He doesn't want to do all the fancy dances and parties. He just wants time with me.

He's the love of my life, and I know it without a shadow of a doubt. He's been my everything for so long that my best friend has convinced me he's going to propose tonight so we can start the next chapter of our lives together.

He's been acting a little weird the last few days, but if he were planning a proposal, that would make sense. So I took extra care getting ready this evening, doing my hair and makeup the way he loves. I even have a new dress for the evening.

We're meeting at the lake that has been our spot out on the dock. I have images of a beautiful, picturesque proposal with candles all over the place as he stands and waits for me.

When I arrive, the only light is from the lamp post on the shore, but Ethan's at the end of the dock, staring out into the lake. I take a moment to gaze at him. He still gives me butterflies after all this time.

He's always been aware of his surroundings, so I know he hears my footsteps, but he doesn't turn until I take the first step onto the dock. His expression is serious. He doesn't smile, and there's a haunted look in his eyes. Something's wrong.

As soon as I reach him, I take his hand in mine to offer him a bit of strength. "What's wrong? Is everything okay?"

His eyes wander over me for a moment before he shakes his head. "I need you to know that I wanted the life we planned, but I have no idea how to give it to you."

"We don't have to figure out how to get there yet. It will take time, and we can do anything together."

Ethan shakes his head again. "I decided to join the Navy. I leave in two weeks for basic training."

He drops the bombshell and then watches and waits for my reaction.

We were supposed to get an apartment together, live together, go to school together, start our life and plan the rest of our life together. The military was never part of that plan.

My mind races as I try to adapt to the new plan. "Okay. As soon as you get stationed, let me know, and I'll transfer my classes. How long is basic training? Will I be able to write you? Can we talk? Is it like the movies, where I won't hear from you for eight weeks? It's sucks, but we'll make this work. They provide housing, right? So we can live in the military housing while I go to school, and you start working."

"No, Bri. I don't want to do the long-distance thing. It's hard enough being away from you for a short time. We won't last long distance. This is for the best for both of us. We end here and go our separate ways.

I'm in complete disbelief. "You can't be serious. This is us. We can work through anything. Listen, my parents are gone for the night. Come back to my place, and we can work through this."

He looks over my head and sighs. "Okay, let's go back to your place."

Once there, we head straight up to my room. I don't get a word out before he kisses me and pins me against the door. My mind goes blank.

We rip at each other's clothes, tearing them apart before he grabs my ass and picks me up. I wrap my legs around his waist, and he carries me to the bed.

In one movement, he lays me down and slides inside me. We moan at how good it feels to be connected. He makes love to me fast and desperately. His lips stay on mine like he's afraid of what I'll say if he stops. Hell, I'm afraid of what either of us will say.

My orgasm is fast and intense and hits me out of nowhere, causing me to cry out. He follows me over the edge and then holds me. I feel so safe in his arms.

When I wake up the next morning, I'm tucked into bed, but Ethan and every sign of him is long gone.

The note on my nightstand is the only sign he was here.

Bri,

I love you with all my heart and always will, but I meant what I said.

I won't force you to do a long-distance relationship, so it's best we end here.

I don't have the same options you do. You're going to do amazing at that big school, but we were lying to ourselves to think I had the grades to join you.

You're going to do incredible things, and you're going to find someone worthy of standing by your side.

It just can't be me.

Ethan

My heart shatters into a million little pieces. In the blink of an eye, the love of my life and my best friend is gone.

I can't get out of bed, and I can't eat or sleep.

Days pass. After a week of refusing to change out of his T-shirt, my dad walks into my room, throws me over his shoulder, and tosses me into a cold bath, telling me I stink.

I don't have the energy to move. I sit and let the water soak me to the bone. My mom walks in, helps remove my clothes, and bathes and washes my hair. I find the strength to pull on a T-shirt and crawl back into bed.

Two weeks pass without a single word from Ethan. I know he's at boot camp, and the thought makes me sick. The thought of him getting on that bus and leaving me has me running to the bathroom and throwing up what little food is in my stomach.

I spend two nights on the bathroom floor, the room spinning as I throw up everything I force myself to eat.

Eventually, I pass out and wake up in a hospital room. My mom and dad sit on either side of me, each gripping a hand.

"What happened?" I ask, remembering falling asleep on the bathroom floor.

"You wouldn't eat or drink. You were so sick, and when we tried to wake you up, we couldn't, so we rushed you here. They got you started on fluids and some food. Why didn't you tell us you were pregnant?" my mom asks with tears streaming down her face.

Pregnant?

There's no way. We were always so careful… until that last night together. In our wild frenzy, I don't think we used a condom.

"I didn't know," I whisper as I lie down, close my eyes, and start to cry all over again.

Chapter 2

Ethan

Present Day

This sure as hell was not part of the plan. I didn't have any other options when I joined the Navy. I figured it was one of the safest bridges in the military. I could do my time going to school, retire after twenty years, and figure out what I wanted to do with my life.

I wasn't supposed to be on the ground during deployment, and I sure as hell wasn't supposed to be injured—an injury that unexpectedly ended my career.

I spent months healing at Oakside military rehabilitation center. Now I'm going home to figure out what comes next. My dad owns a construction business and is always looking for help, so he'll give me a job while I figure it out.

I know what coming into town means and the people I might run into.

Bri.

She's never been far from my mind. I try to picture what she's doing and if she's happy. I hope she met someone who gave her everything she deserved. I hope she has the life she always wanted, even if it kills me that she has that life with someone else.

There's never been anyone else for me, and I know there never will be. That's why I know I can't stay here. I can't watch her live out our life with someone else. This is a pit stop for me to make plans and figure out my life.

It's been a long night of driving, and I'm exhausted, so I stop at the local diner to grab some breakfast and coffee before I head to my parent's place.

I step in and head straight to the counter, and a hush falls over the diner. After placing my order, I notice everyone is looking at me. You could cut the tension in the room with a knife. A few people are staring at a booth by the window. I follow their eyes, and that's when I see her.

Bri is sitting at a booth with her parents having breakfast. But that's not what catches my attention. No, I can't take my eyes off the little boy sitting next to her who looks like me.

Bri sees me, and her eyes go wide. Suddenly, I have a million questions.

Is that my son?

Did we create a life together?

Why didn't she tell me?

Why the hell would she keep something like this from me?

Without thinking about it, my legs move toward their booth.

"Bri." I greet her, ignoring everyone else at the table.

"Ethan. This is the last place I expected to see you," she says.

I can hear the hurt in her voice. "I'm home for a bit. I'll be working for my dad."

"What about the Navy?"

There's a wall between us, and she's determined to keep it there.

"I was injured and medically discharged. Who's this?" I nod at the little boy next to her.

That's when she drops any pretense of being civil. "It was nice of you to come over and talk to us, but we were just leaving," she says, her voice cold and distant.

It's obvious they weren't done eating. Everyone's plate still is half full, and the little boy looks devastated that he can't finish his pancakes.

"But Mom..." he whines.

"I said we're done," she snaps.

The little boy instantly stops, like he's not used to being snapped at like that.

Bri's parents stand, and her dad tosses some money on the table. Not another word is spoken as they walk past me and out of the diner.

What the hell just happened?

Not only did they not finish their breakfast, but a glance at the table reveals her dad left a fifty dollar bill for a meal that didn't cost twenty dollars. They were in such a hurry to get out of here that he didn't even wait for change.

"Ethan, your food's ready," the lady behind the counter calls.

I turn, and every eye in the diner is on me. Like they're waiting for a big reaction to shocking news. It's extremely unsettling.

I make my way to the counter and pay for my food, leaving a generous tip before heading out the door.

I debate going over to Bri's house to get some answers, but it didn't seem like she wanted anything to do with me. I can't blame her. Most days, I don't want anything to do with myself for what I did to her. For what I did to us.

I head to my parents' house, hoping it'll be my safe haven.

Chapter 3

Bri

It's been five years since I saw Ethan. Five years since he set foot in this town. The last thing I expected when I agreed to meet my parents for breakfast was to run into my son's dad.

A dad who has no idea this little boy even exists, no matter how hard I tried to reach out and let him know. Letters upon letters returned to sender unopened. He never had social media, so no matter how hard I tried, I couldn't find him.

I hoped the news of a baby would open his eyes, and he'd realize that walking away wasn't the right thing, but my heart broke with every returned letter. I finally realized I was on my own and became okay with that. I love my son more than I love life, but I always knew this day would come.

But I wasn't counting on seeing Ethan and having my heart skip a beat. My body remembers what it was like to have his hands on me, his lips on mine, and him inside me.

It's easy to remember what it was like to be loved by him. It's easy to feel like that eighteen-year-old girl again, wrapped up in us. But I remind myself there is no us, not anymore.

My feelings for him never really went away. They've always been there on the surface. They were there the day our son was born. They were there when I tried to go out on a few first dates while I was in school, and they were there the night I got drunk on my twenty-first birthday and thought I saw him across the room.

And now those feelings are clouding my judgment. I don't need anyone to tell me that, but I know I'll get an earful as soon as I get home.

At least my parents had my back in there. I don't think they wanted to see him anymore than I did. I know my father sure as hell didn't want a confrontation in the middle of town.

My parents are waiting in the living room when I step in the door after taking a long way home. After I found out I was pregnant, my parents and I had many long talks. One of them was that they wanted to be part of their grandson's life and me to finish school to give him the best life possible.

For that reason, I continued to live with them. I postponed starting college by a year, and I graduated. My parents insisted I find a job and get settled before trying to find a place. I'm sure they don't want Blake to leave because they've gotten attached to him.

"Blake, go play in your room, please," I tell him, and he runs off without question.

"Did you know he was in town?" my mom asks.

"I had no clue. Last I knew, he was stationed in Virginia, but I could never get the specific details," I tell them.

"You can't let your feelings toward him affect your actions," my dad says.

For the longest time, I was heartbroken over Ethan. But after our son was born, I was angry that he wasn't a part of our son's life. My parents sent me to therapy, which helped release my anger because that wasn't healthy for Blake or me.

"I don't know what to do," I admit as I sit on the couch next to my mom.

She scoots over and wraps me in a warm hug. At moments like this, I hate being an adult.

"He deserves to know the truth. He needs to hear it from you and not from someone in town. People may not talk about it, but they've put two and two together. They know who Blake's father is even if you've never said it out loud." my mom says.

I know she's right. The people in this town have rallied around us, and although they don't bring it up, it doesn't mean they don't know.

"Will you keep an eye on Blake? I'm going for a walk around the block to clear my head and try to track down Ethan. It's a conversation I don't want Blake to overhear," I say as I stand.

"Of course, baby. I'll call Mrs. Owen and see if she's heard where he's staying, and I'll send you a text," mom says as I head out the door.

Mrs. Owen is the town's busybody and acts like a grandmother to everyone. She owns a knitting shop on Main Street but doesn't do much work. She likes to sit in a rocking chair out front and knit while watching everything.

I walk down the street toward the quiet little City Park. It has a lake nearby where I love to sit and relax when I need a few minutes. It also has Blake's favorite playground, so that helps too.

I get to the park and sit on a bench overlooking the small pond. I have no idea how to begin sorting out my thoughts.

After a few minutes, my phone pings with a text.

Mom: Ethan is staying in a rental a few blocks from his parents. Here are the phone number and address.

Leave it to my mom to figure it out so quickly. I know she sent both so I can decide if I want to do this over the phone or in person. I figure over the phone because it's easier to hang up if things don't go well.

I save the information my mom sent me and dial Ethan. After the first ring, I hang up, not ready to hear his voice, much less have this conversation.

I take a few more deep breaths, reminding myself that I've raised my son these last four years. I carried him and gave birth to him. I can do this for him.

I dial the number again.

Chapter 4

Ethan

I have breakfast with my parents and then go to my place down the road to start unpacking. My mom carried the whole conversation, and I didn't mention running into Bri, though I'm sure she'll hear all about it before the end of the day.

I've been moving boxes into the relevant rooms while my brain processes what happened at the diner. I'm so lost in my thoughts it takes me a moment to realize my phone is ringing.

I look down and see a number I don't recognize. It's local, so maybe someone's calling to say hi and decide to answer it.

"Ethan? It's Bri," the soft voice I'd know anywhere says.

"Bri." I sigh because hearing her voice is soothing no matter what the situation is.

"About earlier. I didn't know that you were home."

"I just got into town. My stuff arrived a couple of days ago," I tell her, trying to keep it friendly.

"How long are you in town?"

"A while. I'm going to work for my dad for a bit."

"What happened to the Navy?"

For a moment, it feels like things are back to how they used to be. Talking to Bri was always easy, and she truly cared about what was going on in my life. I haven't had that since her. She was my best friend, and I lost that the day I broke us.

"I was injured on my last appointment and medically discharged." I cringe, waiting for her to ask the question everyone asks.

"Are you okay?" Her voice is full of concern.

It's not the question I was expecting. Everyone always wants to know what happened. They want the details as if I'm perfectly okay talking about them. I should have known, though. That's not Bri. She won't ever push me to talk about something. She just wants to know I'm okay.

"I am now. Or I was until I walked into that diner." I try to get the conversation back on track.

Bri goes silent at the end of the phone.

"Come on, Bri. We've never had secrets between us. Is he my son?"

She gives a bitter laugh. That's so unlike her. "Yeah, he's yours. I found out after you left."

My whole world stops and tilts. I have a son. Bri and I have a son. Holy shit, I'm a dad. "What..." I stop and clear my throat. "What's his name?"

She takes a shaky breath like she's scared of my response. "Blake."

I swear the world stops spinning for just a moment.

How many nights did we lie together, plan our future, and the life we wanted? We talked about everything—where we wanted to live, what we wanted to do, how we wanted our house to look, and even our children's names.

I told her I'd always wanted a son named Blake after my little brother, who was born premature and died on his first birthday.

Neither of us says anything right away. We just soak at the moment.

"Would you like to meet him?" she whispers.

"Yes. When? Where?" I say immediately.

"Tomorrow, if that works. At the little park down the road from my parent's place, the one where we used to walk to with the little pond. Ten am?"

"I'll be there. Should I bring anything? What does he like?" My nerves suddenly hit in full force.

"You don't need to bring him anything. He'll have a blast playing at the park. You can ask him what he likes when you see him tomorrow. Goodbye, Ethan," she says and ends the call.

I'm beyond excited for tomorrow and immediately call my mom. I relay the entire day's events, but I don't get the reaction was expecting when I tell her about Blake.

"How can you be sure the kid is yours?" she asks abruptly, throwing cold water on me and ruining my mood.

I know in my gut that little boy is mine. He looks like I did at his age. I know Bri would never cheat on me, the same way she knows I'd never cheat on her. We had an unbreakable level of trust. Until I broke it by leaving.

"I'll get a DNA test, but if you saw the little boy, you'd have no doubt he's mine."

"I have every doubt," my mother replies, her voice cold.

She cuts the conversation short, telling me she has to go and make lunch for my dad. Her attitude strikes me as odd, but my parents have been a little off lately. I put it down to my injury and all the stress it caused.

My phone pings with a notification, and I see it's from the social media app I joined. I'm not a huge fan of them, but I joined to keep in contact with the guys I served with.

It's one of my buddies checking in on me. After responding to him, I wonder if Bri has a social media account. A quick search shows she does. Flipping through the public posts, I see photos of Bri and Blake all the way back to the day he was born.

There are photos of everything I missed, and the more I look, the more upset I become. I can't believe I didn't know I had a son. I should have known. I never would've left if I knew she was pregnant, or if she found out after I'd left, I would've been back every chance I had. I wouldn't have left her to take care of him on her own. There were so many times I could have come home on leave, and I wouldn't have missed the first four years of his life.

The more I flip through photos, the angrier I get. There's no excuse for Bri not telling me about my son, and she and I will have it out tomorrow because I have no intention of missing another moment.

Chapter 5

Bri

Blake was beyond excited when we found out we were going to the park. Of course, he's excited anytime he can be outside at the park. We head out early so we can get there before Ethan. No sooner does my butt hit the park bench than Blake asks to play.

"Please, Mom. Can I go over there where they're playing basketball? Please, please, please?" He points to the basketball court where several kids from the neighborhood are playing.

"Yes, but stay where I can see you, okay?"

"Promise. Thanks, Mom!"

I sit and watch him play for a bit when a figure catches my attention, and I turn to watch Ethan approach. He looks nervous and unsure as he sits at the opposite end of the bench.

"You look terrified." I tease him a little, but I guess it hits too close to home.

"I faced terrifying drill instructors and didn't even flinch, but facing a little boy is almost too much," he says, staring at the basketball court.

"He's going to love you. You'll see," I reassure him. "Blake, come here for a minute!"

Blake says something to the guys he's playing with before running over to me. When he sees the man standing beside me, he stops short. "You're my dad!" he says with a huge smile.

I made sure Blake knew who his dad was. I showed him photos, told him stories of us growing up, and always answered any questions he had.

Ethan is speechless. He looks over at me. "He knows who I am?"

"Of course. I showed him pictures of you, and he has a photo of you by his bed." I smile even though smiling is the last thing I feel like doing.

"Are you done fighting the bad guys so you can come home now?" Blake asks innocently.

"He knows you're in the Navy, and I told him you couldn't be here with us because you're fighting the bad guys to keep us safe."

Ethan leans forward, rests his elbows on his knees, and places his head in his hands before looking up at our son. "Yeah, I'm home for good," he says, his voice thick with emotion.

Blake launches himself into his dad's arms, giving him a huge hug. Ethan is shocked for a second before he wraps his arms around his son and holds him tightly. He buries his face in Blake's neck, and his shoulders shake.

"It's okay, Dad," Blake says, and tears burn my eyes.

"I missed you so much," Ethan tells him, hugging him close.

Blake's friends from the basketball court start calling his name, and Ethan reluctantly lets him go. "Go and play with your friends. Your mom and I are going to talk for a bit."

Blake nods and runs off.

"Why didn't you tell me you were pregnant? Or, at the very least, reach out and let me know I had a son?"

Is he serious? "As soon as I could get out of the house, I visited your parents. Your mother swore to me left and right that she would let you know and you'd reach out to me. I sent letter after letter to the base where you were stationed, but they were all returned to sender."

I pause as Ethan shakes his head in disbelief. "That was just before Blake was born. I gave your mom a photo of him from the hospital to send to you, and she swore she would. About two years ago, I found out you were stationed at a different base. I sent more letters, but they were also returned to sender. There was only so much I could take before I just gave up. I figured you wanted nothing to do with us."

I've only seen Ethan this mad and upset one other time in my life, but even that is no match for the anger I see on his face now.

Chapter 6

Ethan

I'm beyond fuming at my mother. I understand if she had doubts that Blake was mine, but she had no right not to tell me. Even if this little boy isn't mine, I still have the right to know. It wasn't her decision to make.

But I know Blake is mine. I have no reason not to trust Bri. I was the one who broke our trust. If she says this little boy is mine, I know he is. If she says she did everything she could to reach out to me and let me know, I believe her.

"Can I take him out for the afternoon? Maybe for dinner? You could pick him up afterward?" I ask, wanting to spend some time with him.

She hesitates and bites her bottom lip like she used to when she was unsure or uncomfortable about something. I get it. Her job has been to protect this little boy, and she's had to do it alone.

"I'm still the same person. I'll protect him with my life," I reassure her.

Bri's beautiful green eyes lock with mine. "I know you will. In all honesty, it's up to him."

Bri calls Blake over to ask him if he wants to spend the rest of the day with me. He jumps at the chance, bouncing up and down with excitement.

My mind races as I figure out how we can spend the day. I wish things were different with my mother because I'd love to take him there so he can meet his grandparents. But judging by my momma's reaction, I doubt he'd be welcomed, and I refuse to put him in that situation. This little boy is more loved than he realizes, and I won't let him think otherwise. He's a part of Bri and me, the best parts of us.

Blake says goodbye to his mom, races to my side, and takes my hand in his. A vice clamps around my heart at the small gesture.

"You have my cell phone number. Call me if you need anything, or text if you have any questions," Bri says.

"We got this, Mom.," Blake assures her, and I can't help but smile because he's so much like his mother.

"So, one of my favorite things growing up was mini golf? You up for it?" I ask him.

"Yes!" Blake jumps up and down.

We spend an hour at the mini golf course having a blast. Blake tells me about his preschool, friends, his days with his grandma and grandpa, and all his favorite things.

He asks about my time in the Navy, and I give him a clean version of what happened. I take him out for an early dinner at his favorite place, where he runs into some of his friends and is beyond excited to introduce me as his dad.

After dinner, we head back to my place, where he falls asleep. I settle him on the couch, making him comfortable before texting Bri a picture.

Me: He fell asleep on the way to my place.

Bri: I'm on my way. Hope you two had a good time.

Me: We did. Thank you for this. It means a lot to me.

Fifteen minutes later, Bri pulls into the driveway. I head outside to meet her, wanting to talk to her away from Blake on the off chance he wakes up.

"How did it go?" she asks when she joins me on the front porch.

"Great. We talked and got to know each other. After mini golf, we walked around for a bit and had dinner. I'd like to know where we go from here. I want to be part of my son's life. I'm back in town, and I'm not going anywhere, Bri."

"I'm sure Blake will want you to be part of his life after today, and that's all I've ever wanted. What would best work with your schedule?"

I sag in relief that she's not going to fight me on this.

"I'm working with my dad, so my days are pretty flexible. I'd like to spend some weekend time with Blake to do stuff. But I can pick him up during the week if that helps you out. Whatever you need, I want to help."

"It'll take time to get into a good routine that works for both of us, so please be patient. But I have something for you."

Bri reaches into her bag, pulls out a book, and hands it to me.

I take it and open it. It's a scrapbook of photos, memories, dates, and notes about Blake. Pictures and dates of his first smile, his first tooth, his first steps, and more. I look at every page, which goes all the way up to a play his preschool class put on a couple of weeks ago.

"I started putting it together because part of me knew you wouldn't want to miss out on this. I hoped I'd have the chance to give it to you at some point."

I lean in and kiss her impulsively, overcome with emotion. She's unmoving for a second before she kisses me back. It's like no time has passed. Her lips feel and taste the same as they did all those years ago.

She still melts when I cup the back of her head and leans into me when I bite her bottom lip lightly.

But she pulls away all too soon.

I don't want to stop kissing her, but I'm willing to play the long game.

Chapter 7

Bri

Two Weeks Later

Things have been going great as Ethan and I have worked out our co-parenting schedules. My parents miss all the time they used to have with Blake, but they're thrilled that Ethan is in his life. Blake is in heaven, having so much attention focused on him.

Ethan and I are getting closer, and we've been getting to know each other again. Five years is a long time, and a lot has changed, but we're still the same in all the important ways. No matter how great it is, I'm trying not to get too close because I can't have my heart broken again. I can't fall apart like that again. Not now I have Blake to consider.

Ethan still hasn't said a word about his injury and why he was medically discharged. I won't push him. It needs to be his choice, but if we're going to rebuild our relationship, he has to open up at some point. When he's ready, I'll be here to listen.

Ethan picked Blake up from preschool today, and they spent the day together while I was at work. When I arrive at Ethan's to collect him, I don't even get a chance to knock on the door before it opens.

Ethan steps out on the front porch and gives me a quick kiss. "He's at the dining room table with the play dough, so we have a few minutes. I was hoping you'd let me take you out for dinner tomorrow night."

My parents would be happy to watch Blake, but I don't know if dinner is such a good idea.

"We haven't had much time alone, Bri, and I'd like to spend some time with you. Even if things between us don't go any further, I'd like to get to know you as the mother of my child. I want to make sure you're comfortable around me. I also want to thank you for doing such an amazing job raising our son."

I shouldn't be spending any extra time with him, but how can a girl say no to a dinner invitation like that? I want to get to know him again, and wouldn't a good mother do that? A good mother would get to know any person around their kids, so I'd be a bad mother by not going, right?

"Okay. Let me check with my parents and make sure they can watch him for a night."

A brilliant smile lights up his face, and I quickly look away. That smile got me into a lot of trouble when we were together. I remember doing anything to see that smile, and it turned me on so damn much.

When I get home, I send Blake to wash up for dinner. I call my parents to ask them about watching him one night later this week, and they jump at the chance.

"We've missed our one-on-one time with him. It's great he's getting to know his dad, but this is perfect because we'll also get to spend some time with him," my mom says, making me feel better.

Ethan insists on us dressing up and picks me up at my parent's door like he did all those years ago for our first date. He walks me to his truck, opens the door, and helps me in—the whole nine yards.

"So where are we going?" I ask, assuming we're heading out of town because there aren't many places to eat here.

A huge smile crosses his face. "You'll have to wait and see."

He drives to the next town over, to the same restaurant where we had our first date. He's even reserved the same table.

"It was lucky for us before, and I hope it'll be lucky for us again," Ethan says, shrugging like it's not a huge deal that he remembered the details.

We spend the night flirting, talking, reminiscing about old times, and having an all-around great time. Ethan constantly finds ways to touch me, whether holding my hand across the table or touching my cheek. But things get serious when our dessert arrives.

"There's one question I keep waiting for you to ask, I wish you would, so we can get it out of the way," he says, the vulnerability clear on his face.

"What question?"

He sits back in his chair. "Why I was medically discharged."

The cloud of our past hovers over us, dimming the joy of our date. I know he was medically discharged, but physically he looks fine. He's an older version of the boy I was head over heels in love with.

"I've been trying to focus on the fact that you're safe and you're here. I don't want to know how close I came to losing you," I whisper, my eyes stinging.

He reaches across the table and takes my hands in his. "I was escorting another sailor from our ship to a hospital. He was injured on the flight deck. While we were in the hospital, it came under fire, and I took a lot of shrapnel to my leg and side. They stabilized me and sent me to Germany, where I had several operations to remove as much of the shrapnel as possible. But even with physical therapy, my leg will never be a hundred percent, so they discharged me. Physically, I'm fine. I still have nightmares about that day, and I've got a bunch of permanent scars. But I'm here."

Chapter 8

Bri

I take a deep breath. Ethan's right. He's here. It's been five years, but if he hadn't made it home, if he'd died over there, a big part of me would have died too. It would've been worse than the day he left me.

I tighten my hold on his hands. "I'm happy that you're here and safe. I know the Navy was your plan, but I'm not going to lie—I'm happy you're out."

Ethan's eyes hold mine, and he forces a smile as we finish our dessert. He pays the bill, and we head out to his truck.

"I don't want this date to end. Do you want to come back to my place?" he asks as he opens the truck door for me.

"I don't want the date to end either, so yes. I'll call my parents on the way home and check on

Blake." I glance at the time. "I'm sure he's asleep by now."

Sure enough, a quick phone call to my parents confirms he fell asleep watching a movie them after dinner, and they tell me not to rush home.

When Ethan pulls into his driveway, we sit in his truck for a minute, knowing things will change when we step into his house.

His hands never leave as we get out of the truck, and the second the door closes behind us, he has been pinned to it, his lips on mine.

"You look fucking stunning in that dress," he tells me between kisses, running his hands from my hips to beneath my breasts and back again.

I don't get a chance to respond before his lips are on mine again. I run my hands through his hair like I used to, and his growl tells me he still loves it.

"If you don't want this, you need to stop me now, Bri," he mutters as he trails his lips down my neck.

"I'm not stopping this, Ethan," I say breathlessly.

Ethan grabs my ass and lifts me. I wrap my legs around his waist and my arms around his neck as he carries me through the house to his room, gently laying me in the center of his bed.

"The memory of our last time together got me through everything. The deployments, training, and my worst days. I felt so guilty about having you and then leaving like that, but how can I regret it when it gave us Blake? It gave me the strength to make it through without you," he says, his voice rough with emotion.

I swallow hard, and tears threaten to spill down my cheeks.

We make quick work of removing our clothes, and when Ethan climbs into bed, I see the scars he was talking about earlier. I sit up, tracing the ones at his hip, and he freezes. Each scar is proof that he survived. He fought to live so he could come home to our son and me.

I trace the scars down his leg before looking at him. "These scars only make me love you more for everything you went through to come back to us. I love them all."

Ethan's body sags as he collapses on top of me, caging me in the way I've always loved.

Ethan's lips find mine for a slow, deep kiss. By the time he pulls away, we're both breathing heavily. He trails kisses down my neck, between my breasts, and over my stomach until he reaches my core. He plays my body like an instrument. He hasn't forgotten a single thing that used to drive me crazy.

After five years of no sex, those little things that drove me crazy send me over the edge within minutes. Usually, I'd be embarrassed at how quickly he got me off, but Ethan made it a point to get to know every inch of my body when we were together. Knowing he hasn't forgotten means everything to me.

He takes his time relearning my body, the extra weight, and the new stretch marks. He kisses every inch of me before his lips land back on mine. He grabs a condom and rolls it on before sliding inside me for the first time in five years.

We both moan because it feels so damn good. This is home. This is what I've missed. I want to take my time. I want this to last all night, but it's been so damn long, and even as my body is still recovering from my first orgasm, a second one is building.

This orgasm will be stronger than any I've given myself in the last five years. More powerful than the orgasm he gave me the last night we were together, and we made our son.

Ethan tries to slow things down, but I wrap my legs around his waist and pull him deeper just as my orgasm slams into me. He's right behind me, grunting his release as he buries his head in my neck. Seeing my strong, powerful man lose control with me is the sexiest thing I've ever experienced. I've always loved making him lose control, but this is a whole new level.

We slowly come down from our highs, and Ethan tugs me against him, wrapping me in his arms. As he holds me, I realize he's always been the love of my life, and my feelings for him never faded. If anything, they're stronger than ever.

Chapter 9

Ethan

I cook breakfast after the most amazing night with my girl. Bri's already up and called her parents to check on Blake, telling them she has an early meeting and will be home soon. I must remember to thank her parents for covering for us and giving us this time together.

There's a knock on the door. I'm not expecting anyone, but in a town like this, you never know who will show up on your doorstep and for what reason.

"Can you go get that while I finish up breakfast?" I ask, kissing Bri's head and giving her ass a little swat as she heads out of the room.

Then I hear my mother's voice.

"Of course, you're opening the door as if you think this is your place. Why are you trying to get your claws into him again? You're not going to trap him with your bastard child."

I drop the spatula and bolt to the front door. I don't care if I burn the fucking house down because no one talks to Bri that way, not even my mother.

"All that matters is that Blake is Ethan's son. It's a damn good thing your opinion never mattered to me," Bri says as I reach the front door.

"Ethan was right to get out of town and away from you. There's no way that child is his son," my mother spews.

I move to Bri's side and put my arm around her waist. "That's enough. What the hell do you think you are doing? Blake is my son, and Bri is the love of my life. No one talks to her like that, especially not you."

My mother's eyes go wide for a moment before she recovers. "Have you ever done a DNA test to make sure that child is yours? By the time she came to tell me she was pregnant, you'd been in boot camp for months."

"Because I was so sick and depressed. I didn't get out of bed for weeks, much less track my period. I only found out I was pregnant when I landed in the emergency room because I was severely dehydrated and couldn't stop throwing up," Bri grits. "It was several weeks before I could leave the house to visit you."

My heart breaks at everything Bri's gone through, knowing I caused her so much pain. I don't know how she's forgiven me, but I'm so grateful she has, and I'll make it up to her until my dying day.

"I have no doubt that Blake is my son. Zero doubt whatsoever. And that's going to have to be enough for you, Mother," I say, hoping this will put an end to it.

"No, we'll take Blake and get a DNA test because there will always be people who doubt it because your mother is going to put the bug in their ear," Bri says. "At least with the paperwork, we can prove her wrong."

I hate to subject Blake to it, but I know she's right. "Only if you're sure. I don't need a DNA test to know he's mine," I tell her, ignoring my mother's frustrated sigh.

"I know the truth, and it's time your mother does, too," Bri says, shooting a glare at her.

"Go home, Mother. We'll get the DNA test today, but I don't want to see you until we have the results. Don't show up at my house like this again," I close the door in her face, cutting off her protests.

I lead Bri back to the kitchen and try to salvage breakfast, although we've both lost our appetite.

"Let me get dressed, and I'll head to your parents with you. We'll get this all taken care of now." I give her a quick hug, and we get ready to leave.

As I drive to her parent's place, Bri calls her mom and gives her a brief rundown of what's happening. Her mom says she'll have Blake ready to go when we get there.

At the same time, I'm on the phone with the doctor's office, and they're able to get us in for a rush DNA test. One of the benefits of living in a small town and knowing your doctor since you were a kid.

We decide we'll tell Blake I've been exposed to a virus at work, and we want to get him tested to make sure he's not going to get sick before he heads back to school tomorrow. We don't want to involve him in all this drama if we don't have to.

"Dad!" Blake greets me happily.

"Hey, baby." Bri smiles at our son. "Do you want to go for a ride in Dad's truck? We need to stop by the doctor's office and have a quick test done. One of the guys your dad works with got sick, and we want to make sure that you're not going to get sick before you go back to school."

"But I feel fine, Mom," he protests.

"I do, too, buddy, but I'm taking the test with you. It's a quick swab inside your mouth, and we'll be done," I reassure him.

"You're getting tested too?"

"Yes, the same time as you."

That seems to calm him, and he allows us to get him into the truck.

Thankfully we're one of the only appointments with it being a Sunday, so we're in and out of the doctor's office quickly, and he promises to get the results back as soon as possible.

" I'm going to get Blake home, away from any possible drama. I might keep him home from school tomorrow. I know how your mom likes to run her mouth."

She's not wrong. My mom is one of the biggest gossips in town. Blake doesn't need to hear anything my mother spews over the next day or so.

"Okay, you keep him safe, and I'll handle my mother and the town."

Bri nods, and I place a quick kiss on her forehead before she follows Blake inside.

I hate watching them leave, knowing I won't get to spend any more time with them right now. But the best thing I can do is handle my mother.

Chapter 10

Bri

To say Blake isn't thrilled about not going to school the following day is an understatement. Thankfully, my dad steps in and suggests a movie day. He builds a great Fort in the living room and brings in junk food so they can have some boy time.

My dad is great at making forts, and the one he makes for Blake tops any he made me growing up. When I tell Blake this, it cheers him up pretty quickly. They watch all the superhero movies while I help Mom in the kitchen with some meal prep for the week.

Once we're done, Mom disappears to make a few phone calls. I'm sure she's protecting us from the gossip mill as much as possible. Both mine and Ethan's parents are respected members of the community, so this is definitely going to cause a stir.

Mom hasn't told me what's being said, and that's probably for the best. Ignorance is bliss, after all. Strangely enough, my phone has remained silent—until now.

Ethan: Hey, I'm out front. Can you meet me outside? I don't want Blake to know I'm here just yet.

"Ethan's here. I'm going to head outside and talk to him," I whisper to my mom.

She nods, and I head out the back door so Blake doesn't see me.

"Everything okay?" I ask Ethan as I reach the front of the house.

He's holding an envelope in his hand. "I got the DNA test results back. I'm Blake's father."

"Okay." I'm not sure what to say next. This isn't news to me. Ethan is the only man I've ever been with, so I had absolutely no doubt.

"I showed it to my mom first. She's still skeptical and, for whatever reason, doesn't want to accept Blake. I told her I'm having a relationship with my son and his mother. She can choose to be part of our lives or not, but I'm not going to force her. Her response was she'd have to think about it."

I'm not surprised. His mother never liked me growing up. I never knew why, but I didn't push her for answers.

"How do you feel about all that?" I ask, wanting to know where his head is.

"You and Blake are the most important people in my life and will always be," he says simply.

"So, where do we go from here."

"I didn't break up with you all those years ago because I didn't love you, Bri. I didn't have any options for schooling other than the Navy. But you deserved better than having to wait for me. I was certain you'd find someone in school and move on, that I'd return to town, and you'd be married or at least engaged."

I shake my head. "There hasn't been anyone apart from a few bad first dates."

"There's been no one since you for me, either. I was head over heels in love with you back then, and spending time with you recently has only proved that I'm still crazy in love with you. I love you, Bri."

I melt at his words. "I love you too, Ethan. I never stopped."

"I want the three of us to be a family. I've missed so much time. I don't want to miss anymore."

"I don't want you to either. We can work it out if you need more time with Blake." I'm not going to keep Ethan from Blake so long as they want to spend time together.

"I want more time with both of you. I want you and Blake to move in with me so I can come home to you every day. I want the family dinners. I want to tuck him in and read bedtime stories. I want to climb into bed with you and make love to you all night. Then I want to wake up and do it all over again."

My head is spinning. It's such a big move, but I've been prepping Blake about moving out of Grandma and Grandpa's house soon. I'd planned to get my own place here in town.

"We need to ask Blake, and he has to be okay with it. I don't want to do anything to disrupt him too much."

"I agree. Let's talk to him because if he's not okay with it, I'll help you get a place close to mine so we can spend as much time together as possible."

My heart swells. We're going to make up for all those lost years. And I can't wait.

Chapter 11

Ethan

When we bring up the idea to Blake of moving in with me, he's so excited. There's no hesitation it's what he wants. I want to make it happen as soon as possible. So a week later, I'm moving all their stuff into my place.

When I first got here, I thought it would be too big, but it's what was available, so I took it, and I'm glad I did. It's a rental, not a forever home, but Bri and I have already been looking at a property outside the city limits. We're going to find the perfect place and build our dream house, the one we planned all those years ago.

Her dad's helping me move all their stuff in, and her mom's in the kitchen, cooking and stocking the freezer with foods we can warm up. She's always had quick and easy meals in her freezer, and I love that she's continuing that for us.

Bri and Blake are in his room getting it all set up. We painted it blue a few days ago, and it's had plenty of time to dry and air out. When we move out, I'll have to paint it back to the original color, but it was worth the hassle to see my little man's smile when he walked into his room.

As we bring in the last of Bri's stuff, I stand in the living room and look around. I don't care about the boxes, the mess, or the noise. What hits me is how easily her family took me back in.

Don't get me wrong, her dad gave me the talk that if I hurt them again, there will be no third chance, and I respect that. There's no way in hell I'm messing this up again. Bri and Blake are my whole world, and I'm not giving that up for anything.

I didn't realize until now how much I missed being accepted into their family. I'm a part of their daughter and grandson's lives, so I'm also a part of theirs. I was always welcome in their home and at their dining table. I could talk to her dad about anything, and he often sat and helped me with my homework when my parents weren't available.

I always secretly wanted to be part of this family, and now I am, I wouldn't risk it for anything.

All the boxes are here, and we work on unpacking and putting everything away. More than half of the boxes are Blake's, and the rest are clothes and miscellaneous things from Bri's room.

We left Blake's furniture at her parent's house so he'd have a room there when he visits, and we bought him a new set for our house. The only thing he insisted on was still having sleepovers at Grandma and Grandpa's, which we agreed to because that means alone time for us.

We get most of the unpacking done before Bri's mom sits us down for dinner and helps us clean up before they head home.

The three of us sit on the couch to watch TV. I've got my girl on one side and Blake in my lap, who's about to fall asleep.

That's when it hits me. This is the life that Bri and I planned all those years ago. We just took a few detours to get there.

Epilogue

Briana

Three months later

I grin as I stand in the crowd of people at my engagement party. If you'd told me a year ago I'd be getting married to Ethan, I would've thought you were crazy. I knew Ethan was the only man for me, the only one I'd ever love, and if it wasn't going to be him, it would be no one.

I had a piece of him in our son, and that was enough, but to say he's going to be my husband makes me happier than I've ever been.

We invited pretty much the entire town, even Ethan's parents, who've yet to reach out to mend fences. We'll keep extending an olive branch—they'll take it, or they won't, but we're not dwelling on it either way.

Everyone stops us to say hi and congratulate us. Some people drop in to see Ethan from out of town. Others are here for any gossip that happens to go down.

And I know something's about to go down when Ethan's grip on my waist tightens. I look up at him, and he's staring at the front door of the event hall. His mom and dad have just walked in, and they look uncomfortable.

I can't blame them. The whole town knows how his mom reacted and the rumors she tried to spread. The DNA test was all the proof needed for the town to stop listening to her.

Thankfully, Blake has no idea what happened. He's excited to introduce his dad to everyone when we're out in town. Wherever we go, he introduces everyone to his dad. Ethan smiles like a kid in a candy store whenever Blake calls him "Dad."

"Dad, who's that?" Blake asks.

Ethan smiles. "Those are my parents, your other set of grandparents." He picks Blake up as we walk toward them.

"Why haven't I met them before?"

"They've been busy, but they're here now." Ethan tries to distract him. Thankfully, with Blake's short attention span, that's pretty easy.

"Mom. Dad." Ethan greets them. His tone is cool and guarded.

"Life is too short. I don't like tearing my family apart, and I'd like to fix it." His mom looks extremely uncomfortable as she turns to me. "I'm truly sorry for the things I said to you and about you. I know it's no excuse. I thought I was protecting my son. One day, you'll understand, and hopefully, you'll make better choices than I did. I hope you'll forgive me." Her apology sounds sincere.

I look over at Ethan, who gives me a slight nod. I lean in and hug her, which seems to be what everyone around us needs because the conversation picks back up.

"I forgive you, but I won't forget. You're right. I'd do anything to protect Ethan and Blake, and don't ever forget it," I whisper in her ear. I pull back with a smile, and no one is any the wiser.

She looks me in the eye and nods. Seems we're on the same page, at least for now. Only time will tell.

The rest of the evening goes off without a hitch, and my parents take Blake to their house for the night. That gives us a night to ourselves.

No sooner are we in the door before Ethan is taking full advantage.

Link To Oakside
Rest of series.

· · • • ● • ● • • ·

Want more Ethan and Bri? Grab the **bonus epilogue by signing up for my newsletter**.

Want more sexy military men? Check out Oakside Military Heroes starting with **Saving Noah**

Want more Heart of a Wounded Hero Books? **Check out the website for a full list!**

Other Books by Kaci Rose

See all of Kaci Rose's Books

Oakside Military Heroes Series
Saving Noah – Lexi and Noah
Saving Easton – Easton and Paisley
Saving Teddy – Teddy and Mia
Saving Levi – Levi and Mandy
Saving Gavin – Gavin and Lauren
Saving Logan – Logan and Faith

Mountain Men of Whiskey River
Take Me To The River – Axel and Emelie
Take Me To The Cabin – Pheonix and Jenna
Take Me To The Lake – Cash and Hope

Taken by The Mountain Man - Cole and Jana
Take Me To The Mountain – Bennett and Willow

Chasing the Sun Duet
Sunrise – Kade and Lin
Sunset – Jasper and Brynn

Rock Stars of Nashville
She's Still The One – Dallas and Austin

Club Red – Short Stories
Daddy's Dare – Knox and Summer
Sold to my Ex's Dad - Evan and Jana
Jingling His Bells

Club Red: Chicago
Elusive Dom

Standalone Books
Texting Titan - Denver and Avery
Accidental Sugar Daddy – Owen and Ellie
Saving Mason - Mason and Paige

Stay With Me Now – David and Ivy
Midnight Rose - Ruby and Orlando
Committed Cowboy – Whiskey Run Cowboys
Stalking His Obsession - Dakota and Grant
Falling in Love on Route 66 - Weston and Rory
Billionaire's Marigold - Mari and Dalton
Saving Ethan – Bri and Ethan

Connect with Kaci Rose

Website

Facebook

Kaci Rose Reader's Facebook Group

TikTok

Instagram

Twitter

Goodreads

Book Bub

Join Kaci Rose's VIP List (Newsletter)

About Kaci Rose

Kaci Rose writes steamy contemporary romance mostly set in small towns. She grew up in Florida but longs for the mountains over the beach.
She is a mom to 5 kids and a dog who is scared of his own shadow.

She also writes steamy cowboy romance as Kaci M. Rose.

Please Leave a Review!

I love to hear from my readers! Please **head over to your favorite store and leave a review** of what you thought of this book!

Made in the USA
Columbia, SC
23 September 2024